noodle Bear

mark gravas

WALKER BOOKS
AND SUBSIDIARIES
LONDON · BOSTON · SYDNEY · AUCKLAND

On the first day of spring,
Fox invited all her forest
friends to a party.
Everyone was there
except for her best buddy.

Fox thought Bear had forgotten to come,
so she took a bowl of tasty snacks to his cave.

Bear's cave was a shambles!

He was snoring so loudly Fox had to shout into his furry ears.

Instead of sleeping, Bear had spent most of the winter watching a wacky TV game show called **Noodle Knockout** and snacking on all kinds of yummy noodles.

Fat noodles,
thin noodles,
flat noodles,
crispy noodles,
rice noodles,
egg noodles,
gravy noodles
and his favourite,
fish-flavoured noodles.

Bear wasn't interested in Fox's bowl of leftover acorns, berries and fish. All he could think about was ... **NOODLES!**

He looked in the cupboard.

He looked under the TV.

He looked in his special secret hiding place, but there were no noodles anywhere.

Bear asked his friends if they had any noodles.

Squirrel had acorns.

Beaver had sticks.

Deer had grass.

Too grassy!

Rabbit had flowers.

Too flowery!

So Bear lumbered over to Owl's house.
Maybe he would have some noodles.
Bear shook the tree but Owl was asleep;
he wasn't a daytime kind of bird.

Bear was unhappy. He was hungry for noodles.

Fox suggested catching some fish instead.

After all, Bear was a bear and that's what bears do best.

Bear stood in the middle of the stream and waited for a fish to swim by. But he couldn't stop thinking about noodles.

He lost his balance

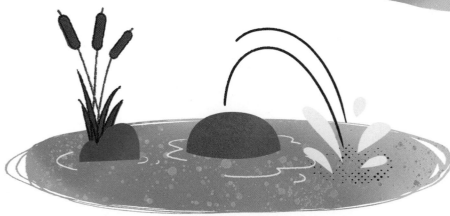

and fell into the water.

Bear decided to go to the big city and become a
contestant on the game show **Noodle Knockout**.
Perhaps he'd win a lifetime supply of noodles.
Fox was very sad to see her friend leave.

It was a long way to travel and Bear couldn't wait to get there.

His log was too slow.

Walking was too slow.

The bus was too slow.

So he hitched a ride with a friendly duck who was also in a hurry. **Bingo!**

It was dark by the time they reached the city.
It was busy. It was noisy. It smelled like **noodles!**

Bear asked for directions to the TV studio.

It was the tallest and brightest building of them all.

Bear joined a queue
of hopeful contestants.

He was picked straightaway because he looked
like a champion noodle eater. **Good choice!**
Bear was very, very good at eating noodles.

He out-guzzled everyone in the **EAT A CUP OF NOODLES** challenge.

He slurped to victory in the **EAT A BOWL OF NOODLES** challenge.

And he gorged his way to first place in the **EAT A BATHTUB OF NOODLES** challenge. Easily!

Bear won week after week and he was crowned the
GRAND NOODLE CHAMPION.

Soon he was a big star.

Bear won week after week and he was crowned the
GRAND NOODLE CHAMPION.

Soon he was a big star.

Bear won week after week and he was crowned the
GRAND NOODLE CHAMPION.

Soon he was a big star.

He had his own cooking show and
all the free noodles he could eat.

But Bear missed the forest, his comfy cave and his friends, especially Fox. He remembered all of the fun things they used to do together.

Swimming in the stream.

Hunting for honey.

And karaoke night.

So Bear went back to the forest.

It was a long ...

long ...

long ...

long ...

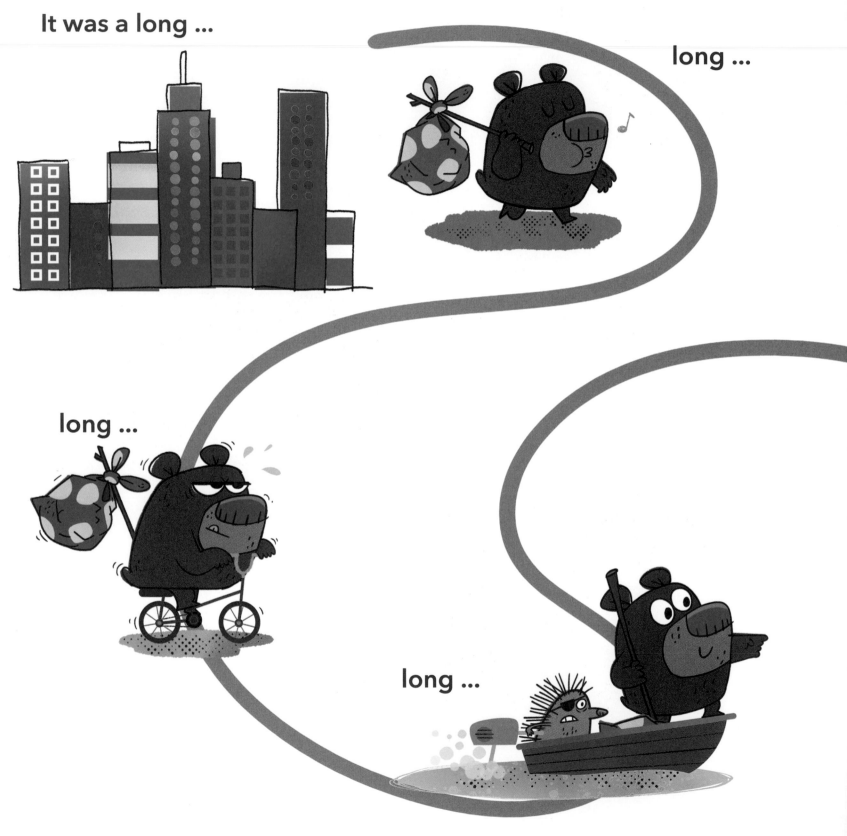

long ...

long ...

long ...

way home.

Everyone was happy to see Bear. Fox threw a big party for him. Even Owl was there! Fox had acorns, sticks, grass and flowers to eat, but still no noodles.

Bear didn't mind at all.
He had enough noodles for everyone!

This book is dedicated to Sandra for her support, even though she doesn't like noodles, and to BTG who knows a lot about bears – and other things too!

First published 2019 by Walker Books Ltd
87 Vauxhall Walk, London SE11 5HJ

2 4 6 8 10 9 7 5 3 1

This book has been typeset in Avenir Next

Printed in China

British Library Cataloguing in Publication Data:
a catalogue record for this book is available from the British Library

ISBN 978-1-4063- 9051-3

www.walker.co.uk